Kestrels 2

A Pony to Jump

Other Patricia Leitch stories you will enjoy

The Kestrels series

1: The Special Pony
2: A Pony to Jump

The Jinny series

Kestrels 2

A Pony to Jump

Patricia Leitch

Illustrated by Elsie Lennox

Lions
An Imprint of HarperCollinsPublishers

A Pony to Jump was first published in the U.K. in Lions in 1992

Lions is an imprint of HarperCollins Children's Books,
part of HarperCollins Publishers Ltd,
77–85 Fulham Palace Road, Hammersmith, London W6 8JB

Printed and bound in Great Britain by
HarperCollins Book Manufacturing, Glasgow

Chapter One

Sally Lorimer stood beside Willow, her dapple grey pony, scowling against the sun as she watched Thalia ("rhymes-with dahlia-which-is-a-flower-like-a-chrysanthemum") Nisbet mounting Tarquin, her finely-bred roan pony. Sally was nine – medium height, not small, not tall; medium size, not fat, not skinny, with thick brown hair, straight to her shoulders and cut into a fringe, wide-set blue eyes and a quirky mouth that turned up at the corners.

"Now watch what I do," Thalia said as she turned her pony and rode him at the first jump.

"What does she think I've been doing?"

Sally muttered to Willow. "All week I've been doing nothing but watch her. I can see what she does but I can't do it."

Tarquin stormed up to the jump, his ears sharp, his eyes glinting. He rose over the stacked wooden boxes in a high soaring arc, leaping as if it was a six foot barricade. He cleared the four other rickety jumps in the same way.

"There," said Thalia. "It's dead simple. You've got to go with your horse. Bend forward just when he's going to jump. Did you see how I did it?"

Sally had only seen the flying speed of Tarquin, and Thalia riding as she always did, with total confidence. No matter what Tarquin did, Thalia sat there effortlessly, her ancient, hardish hat crammed on her sunburst of fair hair; her long, lean body at one with her pony.

"Go on," said Thalia. "Have another shot. And lean forward when Willow jumps."

Sally clapped Willow's neck, remounted reluctantly and trotted her pony in a circle before she cantered at the first jump. Willow took off accurately, popped over the jump and cantered gently on with Sally flopped over her neck.

Sally just did not know what went wrong, but every time Willow jumped she was thrown down onto her neck when she landed. For five days Thalia had been trying to teach Sally to jump and there had been absolutely no improvement.

"Go on! Go on!" yelled Thalia. "Don't stop!"

Willow jumped the second jump and it was only a desperate grab at a fistful of mane that stopped Sally falling off. At the third jump Sally didn't manage to bend forward at all. She was shot out of the saddle at the take off and thumped back into it on the other side. Her sudden weight made Willow's hind legs crash into the jump, knocking it down.

As Willow landed from the fourth jump Sally, left behind again, slid over her shoulder to land on the ground.

"You don't bend your waist," Thalia said, almost shouting at Sally as she scrabbled back to her feet. "You're always left behind. I keep telling you what to do but you won't do it.

I don't know why Willow keeps on jumping for you."

"You're meant to be teaching me," Sally shouted back. "I'm trying to do what you tell me but I can't."

Tears of frustration welled up in her eyes. She wiped them away furiously on her anorak sleeve. "I am *trying* to do what you tell me."

"Then your trying's not up to much."

"And your teaching is rubbish."

The two girls stood glaring at each other.

"Hot pancakes in the kitchen in half an hour," called Sally's mother from the field gate.

She had been taking Meg and Misty, the Lorimers' two Bearded Collies, for a walk on the beach. Coming back she had seen Sally falling off and heard the two girls shouting at each other.

"And lemonade," she added, calling the Beardies and walking on to Kestrels.

Only three months before, the Lorimer family had lived in Matwood, a suburb of Tarent in the north west of Scotland, in a semi-detached brick house.

From the first minute they had discovered Kestrels – empty and desolate and for sale – all the Lorimer family had longed to live there. But it had been far, far too expensive. Then Mr Lorimer's Great Uncle Nathan who had owned a sheep farm in Australia died. Mr Lorimer inherited what his solicitor called a considerable amount of money and Sally's dream of living at Kestrels and having her own pony came true.

Kestrels was a stone mansion house with a high tower, battlements and a courtyard guarded by two enormous stone dogs. It was built on a peninsula – almost an island, only joined to the mainland by a long driveway lined on each side with copper beach trees. It stood surrounded by overgrown lawns, a kitchen garden buried under weeds, a ruined conservatory and a summerhouse perched on the cliffs' edge high above the sea.

There was a stable yard with a feedhouse and tackroom and three loose boxes. The ponies' field, where Thalia and Sally were riding, had been refenced and was now almost perfect, with a stream and a huge spreading chestnut tree for shelter.

For a minute longer the two girls stood not speaking and then they both spoke at once.

"Do you want another jump?" Thalia asked.

"If there's pancakes, I suppose we'd better go in."

They stopped, giggled and the moment was past, almost forgotten as they led their ponies to the stable yard and into the cool, loose boxes, to take off their tack.

Thalia Nisbet was the same age as Sally. Her parents were divorced and she lived with her Narg – Gran spelt backwards. She kept Tarquin at Kestrels, sharing the stabling and field with Sally and Willow.

"Water! Water!" cried Thalia, setting down a full bucket into Willow's box. "I'm going to give Tarquin a feed. Not much. Just a taste."

"And Willow," Sally said, looking critically at Willow as she buried her muzzle in the water, drinking deeply.

Sally had saved her from being sold for slaughter. She had been skin and bone then but her weeks on Kestrels' grazing had rounded her out; giving her coat a healthy sheen and her dark eyes a bright sparkle.

Leaning over the half door Sally watched Willow feeding. She ate delicately, chasing the very last grain of oats round her trough before she turned her attention to the pony nuts.

Sally's heart overflowed with love. Her very own pony. Willow.

"Come on," said Thalia, "or your lot will have finished the pancakes. Sally turned and followed Thalia out of the yard, across the grass and into Kestrels.

She wondered if her mother had seen her falling off. She just didn't know what she was doing wrong. Didn't know why she couldn't jump like Thalia. Perhaps she would only ride, not jump.

"Oh no, Sally Lorimer. You're not going to get caught like that again," she told herself severely. "You want to jump and you are going to jump. So there!"

Chapter Two

All the Lorimers were sitting around or on the kitchen table. The air was filled with the mouth watering smell of newly-made pancakes.

"Here they are," said Emma, as Sally and Thalia came in. Emma was twelve years old, had long, fair hair and could dance and sing as easily as she breathed. "About time too," she went on. "We've all had to wait for you."

"And we're all drooling," added Mr Lorimer.

Jamie, who was four and the youngest Lorimer, brought a tray of pancakes across to the table.

"Watch the dogs!" screamed Mrs Lorimer as Misty jumped up at the pancakes.

Thalia dived and caught the tray, lifting it high above Misty's grey and white head.

"You'd have had a ball with that lot, you fat greedy old pooch," teased Mr Lorimer as he ruffled Misty's long hair over her face, making her bark and leap like a Chinese dragon, her back paws solid, her front paws bouncing up and down, from side to side. Meg, who was an elderly black and white Beardie, sat down stiffly by Mr Lorimer's side, fixed him with her unyielding gaze and began to boof gently but continuously.

"The noise," exclaimed Ben, who was fifteen, wore glasses and had thick black hair like his father's.

Mrs Lorimer brought butter, and jam made from Kestrels' gooseberries.

They ate – Ben hidden behind the local newspaper; Jamie on the floor; Mr Lorimer feeding the dogs bits; Mrs Lorimer telling him not to; Em eating daintily, cutting her pancakes into small pieces; Thalia stuffing herself and Sally having caught her mother's eye and knowing that she had seen her falling off, nibbling round the edge of her pancake, wondering what would be said.

When they had finished washing up Thalia said thank you and that they'd better be getting back to the ponies and Sally began a stealthy retreat to the back door.

"How's the jumping going?" asked Mr Lorimer, freezing Sally in her tracks.

"Okay," said Thalia.

"Didn't look very okay to me," said Mrs Lorimer. "From what I've seen of it you're either galloping madly round on Tarquin or Sally is falling off."

"Tarquin jumps best when he is going fast," said Thalia.

"And Willow? Does she jump best when Sally is falling off?"

"Oh it's not Willow's fault," Sally exclaimed, then clapped her hand over her mouth. She hadn't meant to admit to her parents that anything was wrong.

"Come and sit down for a moment," said Mr Lorimer and reluctantly Sally and Thalia came back to the table.

"Tell us or we can't help you," said Mrs Lorimer.

"Well I keep explaining to Sally what to do but she won't."

"I'm trying," said Sally. "Thalia says I get left behind. Willow jumps absolutely perfectly and then I just sort of collapse on her neck when she lands."

"She won't bend her waist."

"I do. I do bend my waist but it never comes right," and to her dismay Sally felt tears pricking behind her eyes.

"I think," said her mother, comfortingly, "you're needing some help."

"How about jumping lessons," suggested Mr Lorimer.

"There's nowhere. Absolutely nowhere near here," declared Thalia.

"What about Mr Frazer's stables? Surely they give riding lessons?"

"But they cost the earth," said Thalia looking at Mr Lorimer as if he had suddenly gone completely mad.

Sally felt her stomach turn to lead and her heart batter against her ribs. She could not, would not, ever, possibly go near Mr Frazer's stables again.

When she had been looking for a pony they had gone to Mr Frazer's yard. Sally had ridden Bilbo, a sturdy bay gelding with a hogged mane. When the ride had gone down to the sands she had been afraid Bilbo would run away with her. She had tried to dismount, fallen off and refused to get on again. It all seemed a very long time ago and Sally had left the fear of galloping far behind her. She had almost forgotten that she had ever been afraid but her father's words brought it all back – the blaze of the sun on the wet sands, the plunging hooves of the other horses on the ride and the shocked, mocking faces when she absolutely refused to get back on Bilbo. Never could she go back to Mr Frazer's.

"I think I could afford it, thanks to Great Uncle Nathan," said Mr Lorimer. "No matter what he charges it will be better than a daughter in hospital. How often have you come off while you've been trying to jump?"

Sally stared blankly in front of her. She honestly didn't know. She had lost count.

"A few times," said Thalia vaguely.

"Four or five times the day I was with you," said Em.

"Lessons," stated Mr Lorimer. "Most definitely lessons."

"He's got the most super paddock and an indoor school," said Thalia, eaten up with instant jealousy.

"I'm not going, they'd only laugh at me."

"Lessons for you both," said Mr Lorimer.

Thalia made a fish-out-of-water noise. "Me too?" she demanded. "I would totally, absolutely love to go. I never, ever imagined that I would ever have riding lessons at Mr Frazer's. But you can't mean it? Not really?"

Sally sat frozen. Thalia's enthusiasm washing over her in a wave of icy despair.

"Course I mean it. No fun for Sally going by herself."

"Hey," said Ben from behind his paper. "Listen to this. 'Torbracken Open Day. Lady Muriel Spencer is opening Torbracken House to the public on Saturday the sixteenth of August. There will be demonstrations of Scottish crafts, Scottish country dancing, archery, working sheepdogs and many more attractions.

"'In the afternoon the Tarentshire Battlers will enact the legend of the wicked steward who tried to steal the estates and lands of Torbracken from his absent master. Extras are required for this pageant, both foot soldiers, mounted followers and crowd. For further details phone Lady Muriel Spencer at Tarent six-five-four-nine.'"

"We saw them before," said Mrs Lorimer. "The Battlers. At the Abbey Fête?"

"Slashing and stabbing and brandishing," remembered Ben. "They were great."

"Mounted followers?" demanded Thalia. "Do you think they'd want children? Be super if we could be in it."

"Good fun for us all," said Mrs Lorimer.

Sally said nothing. She had seen her father go quietly from the kitchen and she knew what he was doing. He was phoning Mr Frazer, inquiring about jumping lessons. Half of Sally had wanted to run after her father and stop him, for she could not bear the thought of going back to the stables and seeing Martine Dawes, the riding instructor, again. Not after making such an idiot of herself before.

But half of her wanted more than anything to be able to jump like Thalia; wanted to jump with Thalia in the pairs cross-country competition at Tarent Show. And Sally knew that the only way she could do this was to go to Mr Frazer's and find out what she was doing wrong.

"They'd two muskets. KERUMPH! KERUMPHA!" shouted Ben, charging round the kitchen as he tried to explain to Thalia what the Tarentshire Battlers had been like.

"About ten horses and rows of soldiers with pikes at the ready. And in the end they were all dead," said Ben, crashing to the floor and being instantly submerged in Beardies.

"You two could come and be dogs of war," he told them as he struggled back to his feet.

And all the time Sally was sitting perfectly still. Her ears straining to hear her father's footsteps coming back to the kitchen.

"Wasn't there a charge at the end?" said Mrs Lorimer.

"Flat out galloping?" cried Thalia, her eyes shining.

"Flat out galloping charge," Ben told her, grinning at the thought.

"You don't even know if there will be a battle this time," said Em.

"If it's the Battlers there is bound to be a battle," stated Ben. "We *must* be in it."

"That's it fixed up then," said Mr Lorimer, coming back. "A course of jumping lessons for you both on your own ponies, starting tomorrow morning."

"Aren't you star-dazzled with delight?" demanded Thalia as they turned their ponies out.

"No," said Sally. "I'm moon-sick at the thought of meeting Martine Dawes again. And so would you be if you were me."

Before going to sleep Sally sat at her bedroom window at the top of the tower, looking out over the far reaches of the sea. Standing on one of the window bars was a tiny crystal unicorn that she had found before they came to live at Kestrels. It was about two centimetres high with a golden horn and golden tassle to its tail and tiny jewelled eyes that shone dark green and ruby scarlet. Sally had found it lying at the tide's edge. When she put her hand down to pick it up a wave had carried it to her, leaving it in the palm of her hand.

Sally now took it down from the window and stood it in the palm of her hand. In some strange way she was sure it was magic; sure it was the unicorn that had brought them to Kestrels and let her find Willow.

Her new riding things were hanging on the outside of her wardrobe. Very carefully she slipped the unicorn into her jacket pocket.

"Please," she said aloud. "Please don't let me fall off too often and don't let Martine laugh at me."

Chapter Three

Willow and Tarquin – tack polished, well groomed, with manes and tails brushed out into silken falls of hair – trotted along the road to Mr Frazer's stables.

"Be quicker if we rode over the shore," Thalia had said. "But we don't want to arrive all seaweed and sand."

Both girls were smartly turned out. Sally was in her new hacking jacket, cream jodhs, brown jodh boots and crash cap. Thalia was wearing a black jacket, white jodhs and black boots with her faded green-black hat pressed down on her fizzing fair hair.

The sky was azure blue, the morning sun a compact disc of light.

"I think," said Thalia, "your dad might be a saint."

Sally, her stomach leaden, her mouth bone dry, didn't feel she could totally agree.

"Better walk a bit," suggested Thalia. "Or they'll be sweating before we get there."

Slowed to a walk the ponies looked round with a bright curiosity. They knew they were going somewhere special.

"What shall I say to Martine?" asked Sally desperately as the stables came into sight.

"Smile," advised Thalia.

Sally tried smiling but her lips kept settling back into a tight nervous line.

When they turned down the lane to the stables a black mare and her rubber-legged foal came cantering over to them and followed them along the paddock fence. Tarquin's head shot up and, whinnying with sharp puffs of sound, he pranced along beside the mare and foal. Willow, too, danced excitedly behind Tarquin, saying that never in all her life had she seen anything so extraordinary as the foal.

As they rode into the stable yard Sally was too busy trying to calm Willow to worry about what Martine would say to her.

Martine was waiting for them at an open box door. She was wearing a red and white check shirt and navy cords. Her black hair was cut short and her skin tanned after a summer spent working out of doors.

"Has Betsy been showing off her foal?" she asked, coming towards them.

"Think Tarquin wanted to kidnap it," said Thalia.

"All the horses are demented by it," agreed Martine, laughing at Tarquin who was still bouncing up and down like a rocking horse.

"Now, I've met Sally. Glad to see you're riding again. We all have times when everything goes wrong and I guess our ride together was one of those times. So this is your new pony. She is very nice indeed."

Sally beamed.

"And this is?"

"Thalia Nisbet," said Thalia. "And Tarquin."

"Bit of a buzz bomb?" asked Martine, clapping Tarquin's shoulder.

"He's fast," said Thalia. "But that's how I like him."

"And he looks as if he'd have a jump in him?"

"Jump anything," agreed Thalia.

Martine led the way round the side of a row of loose boxes and held open the gate of a large paddock. At the far end were jumps and the other half was a schooling area.

"Before we start jumping we'll do some schooling," said Martine. "You can see letters marking out the track. Ride round at a free walk. Tarquin first and Willow about three pony-lengths behind."

Sally checked Willow until she was far enough behind Tarquin and then let her walk on.

"Sally, relax your hands," said Martine. "Feel the movement of Willow's head through your fingers. If you hold your hands tight and still at the walk you'll catch her mouth at every stride. Relax your elbows. Good. Nice contact, Thalia."

Sally concentrated on her riding, becoming aware of Willow's stride and head carriage. Her seat and hands speaking to her pony. They worked hard, changing from walk to halt, from halt to walk, over and over again.

"Until," said Martine, "you only need to

think halt or walk and your pony obeys."

She showed Sally how to sit straight, looking in front of her and not down at her hands, feeling the collar of her jacket against the back of her neck.

"If you look down you round your back, all your weight goes on your pony's forehand and you've lost the balance we're aiming for."

"Your aids are too sudden," she told Thalia. "You ask Tarquin for a walk and although he knows you so well, he still thinks you might be asking him to spring into a flat out gallop. Gently, easily and sweetly."

Thalia opened her mouth to say she'd always ridden like this but managed to stop herself in time.

They rode at a sitting trot, first with stirrups and then without.

"Best thing in the world for your seat," Martine said, smiling at Sally's expression as she bumped round.

Riding without stirrups didn't seem to make much difference to Thalia but Sally bumped and joggled and held onto the front of her saddle. She was so busy trying to stay on top of Willow that she hardly noticed three girls who were leaning on the paddock rail watching them.

At last Martine relented. "Prepare to walk. Walk. Take your stirrups back."

Gratefully Sally uncrossed her stirrups and, feeling for them with the tips of her toes, was back to normal.

"Practise without stirrups at home," Martine told them. "Remember, sink down in your saddle. Relax. No pinching with your knees. Now, ride round at a free walk. Sally, look up. Then we'll go down to the jumps and you can let me see you jumping."

Now that she was quietly walking round, Sally had time to look at the three girls who had been watching them. She was sure she knew one of them – a girl a bit older than herself with styled brown hair, a spotty skin and a stupid giggle that seemed to get louder each time Sally rode past them. Her friends both had wavy, ginger hair, freckles and pale blue eyes. They looked like sisters and their giggling was even louder than the spotty girl's.

As Martine led the way down to the jumps,

Sally shivered with a sudden grip of nerves. "This is where you fall off," she thought. "Where you make a fool of Willow." She laid her hand on Willow's shoulder and flicked a strand of mane over to the correct side of her neck. Somehow it made it worse always falling off when her pony jumped so willingly.

"Who are the gigglers?" Thalia asked, reining Tarquin in, waiting for Sally to catch up.

"Don't know," said Sally, thinking about jumping; wondering whether it would be better to hold onto a handful of Willow's mane as they cantered up to the jump and flop down onto Willow's neck as they landed or to sit well back and be thrown out of the saddle as Willow took off.

"Well the spotty one knows you. That's what they're giggling about, the toads!"

The three girls were following them down to the jumps. Sally twisted round and looked at them intently. At first she couldn't think who they were, then, with a sinking heart, she recognized the spotty girl. She was the girl who had been out with the ride on a piebald pony the day Sally had fallen off Bilbo and refused to get on again. So that was what they were giggling about.

Martine finished setting up the jumps and came over to them. She looked sharply at the three girls but they paid no attention to her.

"Right," she said to Thalia. "Canter round once and then jump those four just as if you were jumping at home."

Thalia nodded, her face beaming. She touched Tarquin into a canter and the roan pony sprang forward, his ears pricked and his head high, knowing he was going to jump.

Tarquin stormed up to the first jump, clearing it with miles to spare, while Thalia sat tight and close, urging him on. She cleared all four jumps at the same breakneck speed and then it was Sally's turn.

She began to trot Willow round the paddock, aware of the girls' giggling, of Martine watching her intently and Thalia standing beside Tarquin praising him.

"Let her canter on," called Martine, and Sally unwillingly eased her reins a fraction, allowing Willow to canter unevenly up to the first jump. Sally sat back, bumping down on the saddle as Willow jumped.

"Go with your pony," Martine instructed. "Bend your waist."

"Sounds just like Thalia," Sally thought, and leaned forward to grab Willow's mane, collapsing over her neck as they cleared the second jump.

Before Sally had found her balance again Willow had turned and trotted on to the third jump. As she jumped, neatly, willingly, Sally slid over her shoulder. The ground came rushing up to meet her as she fell.

"This is the best bit," giggled the spotty girl. "She won't get on again, you'll see."

"Shut up," said Thalia, turning on them. "Just shut it."

Sally scrambled to her feet, still holding onto her reins, and had remounted almost before Martine reached her.

"And that's what happens all the time," said Sally hopelessly.

"Won't happen again, I promise you." Seeing that Sally was all right Martine marched over to the three girls.

"On you go, right away from here," she told them. "Charlotte, if your tack is still in the disgusting state it was in yesterday, you are not coming on any ride with me. Now off with you. Any more of your nonsense and I'll speak to Mr Frazer about you."

"We haven't time to do much more today," Martine said, turning back to Sally and Thalia. "Your ponies have worked hard and you've done well yourselves. Thalia, you've got to steady Tarquin. Half halts to get his attention. Bring him back onto his quarters and balance him. Small circles at a sitting trot. Changes from walk to trot, trot to walk and halts. Lighten your aids. I'm sure he'd respond to a whisper if you give him the chance."

Thalia listened carefully, nodding her head and biting her tongue to stop herself arguing.

"Sally, it's you, not your pony. We need to work on giving you a firm, balanced seat, so lots of exercises when you're on Willow – toe touching, twisting with your arms outstretched and swinging your legs right round – front, side, back, side and round to the front again. And lots of work at the sitting trot without your stirrups."

"I'll try," said Sally. "Will that really teach me to jump?"

"I promise," said Martine. "Now, when is your next lesson?"

"Not tomorrow but the next day," said Sally.

"Good," said Martine. "We'll concentrate on riding over poles and a small jump."

"Martine! Phone!" called a boy, shouting from the back of the loose boxes.

"Walk them round a bit and then come up to the yard," said Martine, and ran long-legged towards the stables. As soon as she was out of sight, Charlotte and her two gingery friends reappeared.

"What do they want?" Thalia asked suspiciously as she and Sally rode round the edge of the jumping paddock.

"Hi," called the spotty Charlotte. "We want to ask you something."

"Ig-nore, ig-nore," commanded Thalia in robotic tones.

"Listen. We want to know why you were jumping such squidgy, tiny jumps?"

"Were you afraid?" echoed a ginger girl.

"Leave them alone," Sally warned, but

Thalia had already swung Tarquin round.

"What did you say?" she demanded.

"Are you afraid to jump a real jump?" giggled Charlotte.

"Watch," spat Thalia. "Stand there and bloomin' watch me."

The four small jumps put up by Martine were in the middle of the paddock. Around the edge were three jumps about two feet high and one that looked over three feet.

Thalia gathered Tarquin together.

"We'll show them," she whispered. Tarquin sensed her excitement and pranced on the spot; tight as a coiled spring.

They soared over the first three jumps as Sally had known they would. She turned to tell Charlotte and the gingery girls to mind their own business in future, then realized that Thalia had not finished jumping.

"Don't!" Sally screamed. "It's too high! Stop!" Her voice sounding like a high pitched shriek.

She heard Charlotte gasp and one of the gingery girls shout something about Martine, as Thalia rode at the spread of poles.

It seemed to Sally that Thalia was jumping

in slow motion. Tarquin rose at the red and white poles, climbing on air, like a salmon fighting its way up a weir, before he stretched out in a fluid arc and landed far beyond the jump. Throughout all the jumping Thalia had hardly moved in the saddle. Only her hands, light and sensitive, had followed Tarquin's reaching head.

Thalia rode straight up to Charlotte.

"Right?" she said. Then she turned Tarquin to ride up to the paddock gate.

"I never knew you could jump like that!" said Sally, trotting Willow to keep up with Tarquin's long stride.

"Well he is more or less thoroughbred," said Thalia, trying to sound as if it had been nothing, as if she jumped that height every day. But her lips curled up at the corners with pride in her pony.

As they reached the stables they both saw Martine at the same time. She was standing waiting for them, her face coldly furious.

"I did not see what I have just seen. If I had seen it you would go home and never ride here again. Of all the foolish, stupid things to do! Asking an eleven-two pony to jump that height. While you are on our ground Mr Frazer is responsible for your safety. I left you alone because I thought you had some sense, but obviously I was wrong."

"It was Charlotte," interrupted Sally.

"I do not want to hear any excuses. What would have happened if Tarquin had broken a leg?" she asked, looking directly at Thalia.

"Now dismount and lead your ponies up to the yard. Wait there while I fetch a prospectus for Mr Lorimer."

Sally and Thalia waited in the yard, not looking at each other. Thalia biting hard on her quivering lower lip.

A car drove into the yard, and Thalia and Sally moved out of the way. Beside them was a notice pinned to the tack room wall. It was a notice about the pageant at Torbracken House. Any child or adult who wanted to take part in the pageant as a mounted follower was to come to a meeting in the indoor school the next morning when Lady Muriel Spencer would speak to them herself.

"Let's go," said Sally. "We must be in it."

It was Charlotte's voice that replied.

"You needn't bother. It's all more or less

fixed up. The mounted followers are all going to be from here. People who keep their horses here."

"Don't tell me it's you again," raged Martine, coming across with a prospectus and overhearing Charlotte. "You would cause trouble in Antarctica. I don't want to know what was going on in the paddock to make Thalia take such a stupid risk but I don't doubt you were the cause of it."

Charlotte hunched her shoulders and stomped away.

"Give that to your father." Martine handed Sally the prospectus.

"Thanks," muttered Sally, wanting to escape.

"Never again Thalia," warned Martine. "You only jump if I tell you to." Then she grinned suddenly, "But if you're interested in show-jumping I think that pony would take you to the top."

Thalia, who had been avoiding Martine's eyes, gave a gasping, choking gulp, her face suddenly switched on like an electric light bulb.

"We'll see you both tomorrow morning," said Martine as they mounted.

"No," said Sally. "Our next lesson is the day after tomorrow."

"Lady Spencer's meeting. You must come and be mounted followers."

"Charlotte said . . ."

"Don't tell me you're still listening to things our dear Charlotte says?" demanded Martine. "She should be banned from coming here, the trouble she causes."

As they rode back to Kestrels, their ponies' hooves sharp on the road, Thalia was still beaming all over her face.

"I think she is absolutely brill."

"Yes," agreed Sally. "Yes she is." And she squared her shoulders, and looked straight ahead. "I'm going to practise my exercises sitting on the back of the sofa as well as when I'm riding."

"Why not?" agreed Thalia. If Martine had told her to practise jumping while standing on the saddle she would have done it.

Chapter 4

When Sally got down to the stables the next morning, Thalia had already brought the ponies in. She had groomed Tarquin, tacked him up and was just starting on Willow with a dandy brush when Sally arrived.

"Late," stated Thalia.

"Mum burnt the porridge. It was my turn to walk the dogs and when I was all ready Jamie spilled his orange juice over me. So that's why."

"Don't chat, brush," said Thalia irritably.

When Willow was ready Sally discovered that she had forgotten her hard hat and had to go back to her room at the top of the tower for it.

"We'd better ride over the sands," said Thalia when at last they were mounted, and she led the way down the track to the shore. "It saves about ten minutes."

Whenever Tarquin's hooves touched the sand he broke into a gallop. Willow followed. The sea wind blew back their hair and the brilliance of sea and wet sand dazzled their eyes. Sally urged Willow on, imagining herself riding in the pageant. They must reach Mr Frazer's yard in time to be chosen as mounted followers.

As Sally galloped on she gradually became aware of a noise behind her.

"Oh please no. Oh no," thought Sally, not daring to look behind. "It can't be," but unless a wolf pack was pursuing them it could only be . . .

Sally steadied Willow to a trot and forced herself to look back and it was.

Hurtling after them was Misty, her shaggy grey and white coat matted about her in wet, sandy, strands of hair. She was running with her mouth wide open, the baying, barking, howling noise pouring out of it. Her round, yellow eyes were staring at Sally.

Thalia reined Tarquin in and stared in horror as Misty caught up with them and flopped down in the sand.

"I must have left the door open," admitted Sally guiltily as she jumped off Willow. "Quite good the way she tracked us."

"Quite good! The meeting starts in five minutes so we haven't got time to take her back to Kestrels," and Thalia gazed down in disbelief at the mound of hairy sand and the two yellow, saucer-eyes glaring up at her.

"I suppose we'll need to take her with us," continued Thalia. "Perhaps we could shut her in somewhere, but if we don't get a move on it will all be over."

"Why do you always have to be so bad?" Sally said. "Always you!"

Misty grinned and squirmed at Sally's feet, while Thalia found some binder twine in her anorak pocket. Sally knotted it onto Misty's collar as a make-do lead. Misty, puffed-out by her pursuit, was dragged along unwillingly at the end of the binder twine.

To reach the stables they had to ride through the sand dunes. The ponies, high-stepping as hackneys, plunged their way upwards to the road, while Misty burrowed her way along, with only her head visible.

When they reached the stables there was nobody about although the yard was blocked with cars.

"We can't leave them in a box without asking," said Sally, loosening Willow's girths and easing her saddle.

Suddenly there was a burst of applause.

"That's them," said Thalia, pulling Tarquin towards the large sliding doors. "They're in here. This must be the indoor school."

The doors were slightly open. Thalia peered in and saw at the far end of the indoor school several rows of wooden chairs. Facing the audience were six more chairs occupied by two stout elderly men, one young man and three formidable, horsey-looking women. As Thalia watched, the young man got up and began to introduce Lady Muriel Spencer.

"Lady Muriel," announced the young man, "is going to give us a rundown on her plans for her Torbracken Pageant."

"Let me see too," said Sally, trying to get closer to the crack between the doors. "What's happening?"

Just as Lady Muriel started to speak Thalia managed to get her fingers round one of the sliding doors and give it an energetic push. The door swung back on oiled runners and everyone in the indoor school looked round in surprise.

"Glory!" exclaimed Thalia as she and Sally stood holding their ponies like rabbits caught in the beam of headlights.

Martine Dawes jumped up and came running towards them.

"You're late," she said. "Lady Muriel's about to start. Bring your ponies in and hold them. Really it would have been better if you hadn't brought them. My fault. Should have told you."

"Sorry," began Sally when Martine gave a muffled gasp of horror.

"What on earth is that?" she exclaimed.

"Misty," said Sally.

Misty's matted, seaweedy coat had been sugared over with sand from the dunes. Her eyes were wide open and one of her special smiles lifted her lips from her pink gums showing two rows of glistening fangs.

"She likes you," explained Sally. "She only smiles like that at people she likes."

"Are you going to sit down?" boomed Lady Muriel. "Can't possibly get going with all this interruption, don't you know?"

"Wait here," Martine said to Sally and Thalia. "You'll be able to hear okay," and she sat down without closing the doors.

"Are we ready then?" said Lady Muriel. Sally retreated behind Willow feeling that she was speaking directly at her.

Lady Muriel was about six feet tall and looked about seventy years old. She was wearing a bright green, tweed jacket and plus-fours. Her bullet-proof stockings were purple and her brogue shoes and deerstalker hat looked older than Thalia's hard hat. Her weather-beaten cheeks were raddled scarlet and her clear grey eyes gazed out imperiously. Her thin lips were a mouth-trap ready to snap.

"Now that I can make myself heard," said Lady Muriel, leaning on her stick, flashing lethal death rays at Sally and Thalia. "I expect that you are all aware that a week on Saturday is open day at Torbracken and you are all going to attend. You are going to come and pay sweetly for the invitation, for everyone who comes and pays their three pounds entry money will be striking a blow against the monstrous legions of wood worms who are chumbling their way through the very fabric of the west tower.

"We will defeat them," cried Lady Muriel, waving her stick in the air and rousing her audience to cheers.

"But first things first," and Lady Muriel dived into her tweed pocket, brought out a long list written on what looked to Sally like scratchy toilet paper.

"Open all day," said Lady Muriel. "Refreshments in the dining hall, doors opening out onto the balcony, if dry. Craft stalls in the great hall – home baking, fortune-telling, tombola, bottle draw, paint a mug, stitch a tapestry and many more anti-wood-worm activities. Twelve o'clock in the walled garden, Scottish Country dancing, archery demo, sheepdogs, caber tossing, yoga from the ladies in leotards and acrobatics from the boy scouts. Three o'clock the pageant begins. I have written it myself."

The sudden burst of cheering and clapping that followed made Tarquin dance his forelegs, clinking his bit, and Misty throw herself about at the end of her binder twine, barking furiously.

"When the lands and estates of Torbracken were granted by the king to the first Lord of Torbracken for his bravery in battle there was very nearly a terrible mistake. Peter Brewer, an evil steward who had been left in charge of Torbracken House, tried to claim the honours for himself."

Lady Muriel's audience hissed and booed and Misty barked.

"When the king and his followers arrived Peter Brewer stepped forward claiming to be the owner of Torbracken. He knelt before the king, waiting to be knighted, and at that very second the rightful owner returned from battle," and Lady Muriel waved her stick over her head in triumph.

When the cheering was dying down, a tall, bespectacled man stood up.

"Lady Muriel," he asked. "Would you give us some idea of when this took place? The historical setting, so to speak. Who was king?"

Lady Muriel's eyes sharpened to laser beams.

"My good man," she said. "I am telling you about a legend. I have no earthly idea who was king and to be quite frank with you I am not in the least concerned. In our pageant the Tarent Battlers are enacting our battle scene. I have given them an absolutely free hand. As long as there are pikes and swords and banners, I told them, that's the thing."

The man sat down, totally squashed.

"Now the first thing I want to get sorted out is the mounted followers. About twelve or so. Mr Frazer has this in hand. You must all come without horses to the first rehearsal on Saturday and we'll work out a plan of action."

"That's us," said Thalia. "You hold Tarquin and I'll put our names down."

As Sally was about to take Tarquin, Lady Muriel waved her stick in the air again.

"Jolly nearly forgot," she cried. "Anti-woodworm weapon number one. Everyone must attend because the rightful lord is to be played by my great nephew, Nick Ross."

A sudden flurry of surprise swept through her audience. Sally and Thalia looked at each other, not knowing what the fuss was about.

"Despite the danger of being called a doting old woman, I must say the *famous* Nick Ross. He is bringing his showjumper Rose of Sharon with him. I expect you will all have seen them both show-jumping on the box."

For a long moment neither Thalia nor Sally could speak.

"*The* Nick Ross," croaked Sally, getting her voice back first. "And Rose of Sharon! He is my favourite, my absolute and total, super-favourite showjumper!"

"Mine too," echoed Sally. "The most."

"I've posters of him all over my bedroom walls," stated Thalia.

"And we are going to ride in a pageant with him," said Sally.

"To ride with Nick Ross! To really see him riding Rose of Sharon!"

"Can't believe it," said Sally.

"It's true," said Thalia and the whole of the indoor school sparkled and shimmered with the dazzle of rainbows.

Suddenly there came from the stableyard a banshee howling and barking that was worse than a hundred finger nails being scaped down a hundred blackboards.

"Misty!" cried Sally.

Although she still had the binder twine securely wound round her hand, there was no disgustingly filthy dog at the other end.

Sally pushed Willow's reins at Thalia and dashed out into the stableyard.

"Misty!" she screamed. "Misty come here!"

Misty hesitated, looked over her shoulder at Sally, and sprang into the muck heap, where she rolled luxuriously, still barking.

"Come here at once!"

Misty wriggled back to her feet and shook herself. She lifted one cautious paw, considered obeying Sally and in that instant another dog came bounding up.

He was a wolfhound puppy, Shetland-pony size but still a puppy. He had a rough, grey brown coat, was beautifully groomed and wore an expensive leather collar. The dog jumped up to dance circles round Misty, his front legs outstretched, his long thick tail wagging furiously as he bounded and bounced.

Sally stared in disbelief as the two dogs

careered back to the yard. They raced in and out between the parked cars, having the time of their lives.

"Can't you catch her? They're all coming out," cried Thalia. "Martine's got the ponies."

As the doors from the indoor school were opened wider the wolfhound leapt onto the bonnet of a Mini, then over a sports car with Misty running round the cars in desperate pursuit. People either stood staring or began chasing the dogs round, making them more excited than ever.

"Surely that's Muriel's pup?" said a rich fruity voice.

"Must be," replied her friend, "but where did the mongrel come from?"

"Collie, Bearded Collie," said Sally automatically, but no one was listening to her.

Lady Muriel came through the doors into the yard. With one sweeping glare she took in what was happening and with a voice that would have stopped waterfalls in their courses, she roared "*Patrick*!"

The wolfhound puppy stopped in mid leap, whipped round in the air, fled to his mistress and lay down on his back at her feet.

"Car," commanded Lady Muriel and the puppy scrambled to his huge paws and slunk away towards an open sports car. He bounded in and lay in the back with his chin resting on the back of the driver's seat.

"Is that creature yours?" Lady Muriel demanded, pointing her stick first at Misty and then at Sally. "Remove it."

Misty arched her back, lowered her head and tail and moving very slowly, tip-toed her way across the yard to Sally.

"I'll kill you," promised Sally, knotting the binder twine to Misty's collar. "You are the worst . . ."

"Come on," interrupted Thalia. "Better get our names down to be mounted followers."

"Afraid you're too late," said Martine, giving them back their ponies. "They picked the mounted followers just after you went off to find your dog. They only wanted a few. Nearly everybody is to be foot followers. There's a rehearsal on Saturday at Torbracken. I should think your best plan would be to go along then. Two o'clock."

"Is that Charlotte going?" asked Thalia, her voice shaky with disappointment.

"'Fraid she is. She's to be Nick's page."

Thalia and Sally looked at each other in total disgust.

"Go along anyway," encouraged Martine. "But no ponies. And it might be rather a good idea to leave your sand-hound behind."

Feet out of their stirrups, reins loose on their ponies' necks, Sally and Thalia rode back to Kestrels across the sands.

"We must ride in the pageant," said Sally. "Must."

"With Nick Ross and Rose of Sharon," breathed Thalia, and in her mind there was no doubt. They would find a way of riding with Nick Ross.

Chapter Five

On Saturday, all the Lorimers except Meg and Misty, who were shut in the kitchen with three bones between them – because Misty always stole Meg's and three bones meant that there was always a spare one for Meg to move on to – were driving between the beech trees from Kestrels to the main road.

They were all going to the rehearsal at Torbracken House. Mr Lorimer had found a pamphlet about the pageant at his library. It said that everyone who wanted to join in would be welcome.

Mr Lorimer and Ben were hoping to join in the battle with the Tarent Battlers. Mrs Lorimer had brought her water colours, brushes and sketch pad and was intending to paint and keep an eye on Jamie who thought he was going to be a battler with his father and Ben.

Sally was wearing her oldest jeans, scuffed trainers, black tee shirt and her oldest anorak. It was camouflage. She and Thalia had decided that their best hope was to join in quietly with the unmounted mounted followers and then, if nobody noticed them too much, they would be allowed to stay.

Thalia was coming on the back of her Narg's motorbike. Like Jamie, Thalia's Narg was also planning to be a battler but without much hope.

Torbracken House was not far from Kestrels. It stood in an immensity of grounds – woodlands, formal gardens, fields of organically grown vegetables and a walled garden where the pageant was to take place.

Boy Scouts were on duty. As Mr Lorimer turned into the rhododendron-shaded drive a boy scout directed them to the carpark. When they got out of the car in the carpark, more Scouts pounced on them, asking them which part of the pageant they were interested in.

"Soldiers through the woods to the left. The Tarent Battlers will tell you what to do. They are organizing the Charge."

Em was directed to be a dancer and Mrs Lorimer went with her to be general crowd.

"And you?" the Scout asked Sally.

"I'm not sure," said Sally then heard the welcome roar of Narg's motorbike.

Thalia threw herself off the bike and came running across.

"Mounted followers," she said to the Scout and he told them to go to the stable block behind Torbracken House.

"We're not really," said Sally guiltily, as they walked under the sky-touching pine trees towards the stables.

"Of course we are," declared Thalia. "We are if they'd let us. We must ride with Nick Ross."

Already there were about fifteen people waiting by the stables which were rather cobwebby and unoccupied.

"Look out," mouthed Sally. "Charlotte to your left."

"Take action," Thalia replied and they edged their way round the yard until they found a place to wait half-hidden in a loose box doorway, well out of Charlotte's sight.

"Here we are, here we are," chirruped a sharp weasel woman who came scooting into the yard. She had a cotton scarf tied over strawy hair, flat blue eyes and a smile safety-pinned onto her face so you couldn't tell what she was really thinking.

"Let's get things sorted out. I've got all the gen. down here. Right, now, when I call your name would you come over to me."

"Cut the cackle, Daisy," called a stout, purple-faced man.

"Rupert, do not start. Lady Muriel will be here in a jiffy. Serious stuff. She is in charge."

"Sorry, sorry. Only trying to cheer things up. My mistake."

"Right then," said Daisy, struggling to control the clip board and sheets of paper she was carrying. "When I read out your name please come out here. First, mounted followers in the battle – Sean McGregor on Mutant Turtle; Frank Gunn on Moly . . ."

Sally and Thalia looked at each other in despair.

"She won't call out our names," said Sally.

"Wait," said Thalia.

There were four groups of mounted followers. Those taking part in the battle, those who were with the evil steward, the king's followers and the page who was to ride with Nick Ross – Charlotte.

"It should be us," muttered Sally.

"It will be," swore Thalia but it was like vowing to swim the channel when you could hardly manage a breadth of the baths.

When Daisy had divided them all into their groups she told them to stay where they were because Lady Muriel would be arriving at any moment.

"Bet she knows me," said Sally uneasily.

With Patrick lolloping beside her Lady Muriel surveyed her unmounted mounted followers.

"This way," she roared. "And I shall show you where to ride when you have your horses. Everybody down to the walled garden," and marching ahead she rallied them on with a wave of her stick.

Sally and Thalia hung back.

"We'll be king's men," said Thalia. "They're

the biggest group, so perhaps we'll not be noticed."

Sally said nothing. A blind man on a runaway horse in a sand storm would notice them.

Over the years the walls of the walled garden had crumbled away and the stones lay moss-covered and scattered. In some places the wall was only about three feet high. Broad flowerbeds stretched down from the walls to wide lawns. Torbracken House was at one end of the walled garden. Formal paved walks and yew trees cut and shaped like strange creatures joined it to the shaven perfection of the lawns. Outside the walls were several singular chestnut trees.

"That's where the blighters are," Lady Muriel boomed, swinging her stick in the direction of the stone turrets and towers of Torbracken House. "In the west tower. But we'll sniff them out. We'll get them."

Sally shivered suddenly, goose over her grave. She felt sure that Lady Muriel would sniff her out. She glanced quickly at Thalia but she was gazing about her, looking totally at her ease; as if she had every right to be there.

First Lady Muriel lined up those who were to be in the battle, and then the steward's followers.

"Now the king's horses and the king's men."

Three men, two boys and a lady began to walk across to Lady Muriel.

"Us too," said Thalia between her teeth.

For a moment Sally's feet would not move.

"Sally, come on," hissed Thalia. "We've got to be with them."

As she walked beside Thalia Sally felt every eye boring into her and almost before she heard Charlotte's voice she knew it was going to happen; knew what she was going to say.

"Lady Muriel, those two girls at the back. They shouldn't be here. They weren't chosen," and Charlotte's eyes shone with spiteful delight.

"We should be here," stated Thalia.

"Now who told you to come. You're both far too young to be king's men," exclaimed Daisy.

"But Charlotte's young," said Thalia.

"Oh but she is a page, dear" consoled

Daisy. "And you are not mounted followers, are you? So come along with me and be part of the crowd."

Suddenly Lady Muriel pointed her stick straight at Sally.

"You are the child who brought that abomination of a mongrel to our meeting at the stables."

"Collie," corrected Sally. "Bearded Collie. Pure bred. Pedigree."

"Out!" Commanded Lady Muriel. "Away with you."

"But I haven't brought Misty . . ."

"Out," roared Lady Muriel again.

"I'll take them round to be crowd," organized Daisy. "Watching-the-dancing crowd, do you think?"

"We are not any sort of crowd," stated Thalia.

"But of course you are, dear. Mounted followers were all especially picked, and we can't change anything now."

Daisy left them with the watching-the-dancing crowd.

"We're not staying here," said Thalia. "We've got to know what the king's men do, so when we bring Tarquin and Willow we'll know what to do."

"They'll only send us back again," said Sally.

She could see her father, Ben and Thalia's Narg charging about the rhododendrons. Em was standing a little apart from the dancers, singing to an official looking man and woman and her mother was sitting on a garden seat painting, while Jamie, who had not been accepted by the Battlers, sat on the grass beside her eating chocolate.

"It's no good," said Sally.

"Of course it is. Don't be so soft."

Thalia led the way back to the walled garden. They crouched down behind the fallen stones from the crumbling wall, trying to see what was happening.

"Need to get closer," said Thalia. "That's the king's men they're talking to now."

"You'll gallop along the drive," the man organizing the mounted followers was saying. "When you reach here . . ." and the man began to walk away so that Sally and Thalia couldn't hear him.

"Curse him," said Thalia.

"They'll see us if we go any closer."

They both looked round, searching for a place to hide.

"The tree!" Thalia exclaimed. "They'll never see us there and we'll be able to hear everything."

Crouching as close to the ground as they could they ran through the shrubbery to where a huge chestnut tree stretched its looping branches almost to the ground. It was an easy climb and when they had reached about half way up the tree they each picked a branch and sat astride it, leaning against the trunk of the tree. They were completely hidden by the leaves but they could see everything that was happening in the walled garden.

"Listen hard," said Thalia. "So we'll remember; so we'll know what to do at the pageant."

Suddenly there was a banshee howl and scrabbling over the broken-down wall came Lady Muriel's wolfhound. He bounded across the grass and stood with his front paws on the trunk of the chestnut tree.

Lady Muriel came striding up behind him, one bony hand holding up her long denim skirt, the other waving her stick aloft. When she reached the chestnut tree, she walloped at its lower branches with her stick.

"I can see you," she cried, rousing rooks from their tree tops for miles around. "Get down at once! At once, I tell you!"

Sally and Thalia slid and scrambled their way out of the tree. They stood listening to Lady Muriel's rage, then made their way back to the walled garden.

"Crowd," said Sally bitterly. "That's all we are. Just crowd."

And for once Thalia had nothing to say.

Chapter Six

"That was very much better," enthused Martine, as Sally rode over the poles. "You were with your pony all the way."

Sally beamed, running her hand down Willow's smooth neck and clapping her hard fit shoulder.

It was their fourth jumping lesson, four days since their disastrous day at Lady Muriel's. Only three days to the pageant and they were no nearer finding a way of riding in it. Their only cunning, feeble plan was to arrive at Torbracken riding Tarquin and Willow and hope they would be allowed to join in.

"But no way if Lady Muriel and her hound

63

of the Torbracken spots us," Thalia had said gloomily.

"Now Thalia," said Martine when she had altered the trotting poles to suit Tarquin's longer stride. "Your turn."

There were five trotting poles laid on the ground followed by a small jump. The ponies had to trot rhythmically over the poles and then take the jump without changing their stride while their riders kept their jumping position.

"Steady. Drive him on with your seat, gather him together with your hands. Nice, good," encouraged Martine as Thalia rode towards the line of trotting poles.

Sally watched as Tarquin trotted over the poles, lifting his hooves cleanly between them and flipping neatly over the little jump. Sally could see how much he had improved. He had almost given up his mad dashing and Thalia's aids to her pony had changed from sudden kicks into quiet, accurate instructions.

"Excellent," said Martine. "You have both been working hard at home."

"Trotting without stirrups," agreed Sally.

"Numb bums," said Thalia.

Suddenly one of the stable girls came running from the stables, waving her arms and shouting, "He's here. Nick Ross is here!"

"Bit early," Martine said, while Thalia and Sally goggled, wide eyed and speechless.

"Right," said Martine, "we'll leave the jumping until your next lesson. I expect you'd like to meet Nick?"

"Oh yes!"

"More than anything in the world!"

"Thought you might. You can pop your ponies into a box for a few minutes," and Martine led the way up to the yard.

Parked in the stableyard was a brand new, bright-yellow, low-slung car. Coupled to it was a trailer. As Sally and Thalia led their ponies across the yard there was a sound of trampling hooves from the trailer, followed by a shattering whinny. The car door was flung open and a young man jumped out.

"Get up with you, Rosie," he shouted, banging on the side of the trailer.

He was tall with black curly hair, very dark, glistening eyes and a wide smiling mouth. Sally and Thalia recognized him at once.

"It's him!" cried Thalia "It is you, isn't it? Nick Ross? I never dreamed I'd ever see you like this. Just standing there."

"I do it quite often," grinned Nick. "Just stand, I mean."

"Oh but not where I can see you," said Thalia. "When we heard you were coming I counted all the pictures I've collected of you. I've got thirty-eight. Fourteen up on the wall and the rest in my showjumper box. You are my absolute best showjumper."

"Continue," said Nick Ross, smiling down on Thalia. "Flattery will get you everywhere. Music to my ears."

"Put your ponies in over there," said Martine, pointing to two empty boxes.

"And how is Martine?" Nick Ross asked, hugging her to him. "I only gave in to Auntie's nagging because it meant seeing you."

"That," said Martine, "will be right." She was flushed and bright, obviously delighted to see Nick Ross again.

Sally was just as thrilled as Thalia but she

kept her happiness to herself like a precious jewel that she didn't want to share with anyone else.

Willow and Tarquin watched curiously over their half doors as Nick Ross, speaking in a quiet voice, went into the trailer through the groom's door. The front ramp was lowered and Rose of Sharon came down the ramp with Nick running at her side.

She stood in the yard – mighty, four-square, pure white except for the black skin at her muzzle and eyes. She made everything around her seem second rate, not worth having.

"She is looking well," said Martine. "Full of herself."

"So she should be. Won a few pots since you saw her last."

"She's like the Greek marble horses in the British Museum," said Sally.

"Winter and spring mixed together and made into a horse," exclaimed Thalia. "She is the most beautiful horse I have ever seen."

"She has the brains as well," said Nick. "When you're sitting up there pounding down on the wall at the White City, it's not her looks you're thinking about, it's her brains. Isn't that right, Rosie old girl?"

The great white mare crested her neck and blew over Nick's black hair.

"You've got her wasted like all the rest of your nags," said Martine, laughing.

"Well you might be right but better that way than the other. Could we get her settled? Auntie Mu will be here in a minute. I phoned to let her know I was nearly here."

"Ten star service awaits you, Rosie," said Martine as Mr Frazer came back from taking a ride.

"Better not let Lady Muriel see us?" suggested Sally.

"Phooey to her," said Thalia and hurried after Nick Ross to watch him taking off Rosie's bandages and travelling rug.

"Do you remember last year at the Horse of the Year Show when you just beat John Whitaker? That was because I'd all my fingers crossed for you. If I think someone is going to beat you I will them to knock down the jumps and they always do."

"So that's why I've been doing so well, is

it? From now on I shall only jump in events that are being televized."

"If you'd let me know when you're jumping I could sit at home and will you to win," offered Thalia.

"I'll consider your offer. How much would you charge?"

"Nothing!" cried Thalia, shocked at the very thought. "Nothing, of course."

Mr Frazer came over to talk to Nick minutes before Lady Muriel tore into the yard in her scarlet sports car. She swung herself out of the car and ran across the yard. Pushing Thalia out of her way, she flung open the loosebox door and launched herself at Nick.

"So sweet of you . . ." she began as Rosie started back, rearing up and tossing her head before she plunged to freedom through the open box door.

Nick struggled to free himself from Lady Muriel's embrace but Rosie was already out of the box and thundering across the yard.

It was Thalia who sprang at Rosie's head-collar and held on with both hands, refusing to let go even when Rosie lifted her off her feet.

"Steady the lass," soothed Nick as he rushed to grab Rosie. "Whoa the old girl. Settle, settle."

Nick ran his hand down her neck, clapped her shoulder, soothing her fright and instantly she calmed down, gave a gusty sigh and followed Nick back into the loosebox.

"Just like old times," said Lady Muriel cheerfully. "Never could tie up a pony properly. Always chasing after them down the drive."

"Good job you were quick," Nick said to Thalia. "Or I might have been chasing Rosie down the road now. Thank you very much."

"So glad you made it," boomed Lady Muriel as Nick tied Rosie up securely. "Thousands will flock to my pageant just to see you. We will be hock deep in dead woodworms."

"That will make jumping difficult," said Nick, starting to groom Rosie.

"Tomorrow is the dress rehearsal. Quite wonderful the way everyone has rallied to the call. Cannot imagine what the lawn will be like after the Battlers have battled. But, as

I said to Freddie, if we don't exterminate the little blighters they'll eat the house down."

Nick parked his brilliant yellow car and his trailer; spoke to Mr Frazer, then ran across the yard and leaped into Lady Muriel's sports car.

She was just about to drive away when Nick turned round in his seat and shouted, "Nick Ross Fan Club, attend directly."

Sally had turned away, going to get Willow, but Thalia was still gazing after Nick. She raced towards the car. Nick spoke to her in a low voice and the car drove away.

"What did he say?" demanded Sally.

"It's secret."

"Go on," said Martine. "You can tell me."

"I can't. I promised."

Charlotte, who had been dropped off by her mother, said, "Was that Nick Ross you were speaking to? What was he saying to you? You don't know him. Why should he want to speak to you?"

"Thank you for our lesson," Thalia said to Martine, and totally ignoring Charlotte she went to get Tarquin.

"Right," said Sally when they had reached

the sands and were well away from the stables. "What did he say? I'm fan club too."

"He'll be schooling Rosie at seven o'clock tomorrow morning. *If* we're there, he said, we can watch. *If* we're there, he said, we can have a ride on her. *If* we're there, he said."

"What did you say?" asked Sally, filled with utter delight.

"I said, 'though hell should bar the way'."

Chapter Seven

Sally and Thalia stood at the end of the indoor school and watched entranced as Nick schooled Rose of Sharon.

In the enclosed space she seemed enormous – a huge, soaring bulk of white horse. Her feet were shod with "bright and battering sandals", her legs were power-packed pillars of strength, her body large and hard as a table top and her arching neck was crested like a stallion's. She had flat cheek bones, large ears, lustrous black eyes and wide, scarlet lined nostrils. Her mane was pulled and her banged tail fell in a thick cascade around her straight hocks.

When Nick had ridden her at a walk,

trot and canter, he worked on turns on the forehand and haunches; shoulder in half-passes, and reining back. Martine stood with Thalia and Sally explaining the various movements.

"He always was one for taking things slowly," said Mr Frazer. "Pays in the long run."

Nick turned Rosie and rode towards them.

"Still favours her offside," said Martine.

"Dear Martine, only you would notice that," said Nick, grinning and leaping down from Rosie.

"Now who's going first," he asked, looking questioningly at Thalia and Sally.

Sally's heart tightened and a cold shudder ran down her spine. Since Thalia had told her that they were going to have a ride on Rosie, Sally had kept telling herself how lucky she was and how the loathly Charlotte would give anything to ride Rosie but now that the moment had come Sally looked up at the height and power of Rosie and shivered nervously.

But Thalia was already cramming on her hard hat and bustling to be first.

Thalia spoke to Rosie and then Nick gave her a leg-up and adjusted her stirrups.

"Shall I walk with you?" asked Nick.

"Oh no!" exclaimed Thalia. "That would make it a donkey ride."

"Take care then."

At first cautiously and then with growing confidence Thalia walked Rosie round the school.

"Change your rein and let her trot on," called Nick.

Thalia rode across the school, then touched her heels to Rosie's sides and trotted. To begin with she bumped around, but soon found her rhythm and managed to post. She rode with an ear to ear grin, sitting very upright and looking straight ahead.

"Right," called Nick. "We'll let Sally have her turn."

Sally gritted her teeth and swallowed hard. "Don't let them see that you're afraid," she told herself. "Because you're not. Sally Lorimer, you are about to ride a world famous showjumper and all you're thinking about is being afraid. Stop it!"

Thalia sprang to the ground, landing lightly beside Rosie's shoulder. Her face was bright with achievement.

"When the Queen says, 'Arise Dame Thalia'," she told Nick, "it will only be the second best thing in my life. This has been the best."

Clutching towards Rosie's saddle, Sally held out her leg and Nick tossed her up. From the ground Rosie had seemed massive, from the saddle she seemed to Sally like a universe of horse. There was nothing else.

Nick shortened her stirrups, gave her the reins and walking in front of Rosie led the way round the school. Sally supposed that they must be walking because they were keeping up with Nick but it was like sitting on the elephant that she had once ridden at a zoo – you were moving but you hardly felt anything.

"Not quite what you're used to?" Nick asked, grinning up at her.

Sally thought of Willow and of Miss Meek's plodding ponies at the riding school where Sally used to ride when the idea of owning her own pony was no more than an impossible dream, and shook her head hard.

And yet . . . and yet . . . there was something

familiar about riding Rosie. Something she just couldn't quite remember.

Nick stood back with Thalia and Martine and Sally rode round by herself.

"Do you want a trot?" Nick called.

"Okay," Sally shouted back, hating her voice for sounding too high and shaky. She felt in her jacket pocket for a hanky, blew her nose and put the hanky back. There was something small and hard trapped in the corner of her pocket. She felt it curiously, her fingers searching it. It was the unicorn.

"What trot?" said Thalia loudly.

Sally thrust the little unicorn back into her pocket. Squeezed her legs a fraction and had to grab up her reins as Rosie instantly broke into a trot.

Finding the unicorn when she had so completely forgotten about it was like being given an extra special present when it wasn't Christmas or even your birthday. Sally's delight flowed down her reins and Rosie broke into a slow, flowing canter.

She was riding down the long side of the school and knew Rosie would stop when she reached Nick so she sat still enjoying herself, just sat there being carried smoothly along.

Suddenly Sally didn't want to stop. She touched her leg against Rosie's hard, fit side and sent her on round the ring for a second time and again for a third time.

"Steady on!" roared Nick. "That's enough of that! Bring her back here. Slow her down."

Sally tightened her fingers and instantly Rosie was trotting and then walking. As Sally rode her back to the others she lent over Rosie's withers, clapping her shoulder, thanking her for a super ride.

"Thought you'd be taking her over the jumps next," Nick said in a not amused voice as he reclaimed his horse.

"Sorry," said Sally, hardly knowing what it was that had made her canter Rosie. "She just cantered."

"That will be right," said Nick.

"But thank you," said Sally. "Thank you very much."

There was something plucking at her memory, of a white horse that she had ridden before, a horse as powerful as Rosie and as gentle; as well-schooled and as obedient.

Nick remounted and when he had trotted round a few times he took her over three jumps which she cleared effortlessly.

"You are my best and only girl," Nick told her, clapping her neck and slipping to the ground.

Sally and Thalia watched Nick over the box door as he moved quick and confident around Rosie, still trying to find words to thank him properly. He checked Rosie over, groomed her and when he was satisfied tipped a bucket of feed into her manger. Rosie chomped, blubber lipped, syphoning it down.

"How about a cup of coffee?" he asked them and they followed him into a bright, modern kitchen.

Lady Muriel was there. She looked up when she saw Sally.

"Got that mongrel with you?" she demanded. "Don't bring it in here."

But Mrs Frazer winked at the girls and said to Sally that she'd heard that someone had been galloping Rosie round the school.

"I didn't canter," said Thalia, "because Nick didn't tell me to."

But Mrs Frazer was giving them lemonade

in mugs decorated with gnomes and leaves and nobody was listening to Thalia.

"You two will be going to the rehearsal?" Nick asked. "You'll be riding over?"

"Mr Lorimer is meeting us," said Thalia. "We were not chosen."

"What's this," Nick said to Martine. "Are the kids not riding in the pageant?"

"They are not," stated Lady Muriel.

"But surely you can fit two more in?"

"Utterly not," said Lady Muriel. "And if they bring that wretched mongrel anywhere near Torbracken they will be banned."

"Oh really!" said Nick. "I could do with two more pages. Let them come?"

"Nicholas," said Lady Muriel. "Who is in charge here?"

"You are," said Nick, grinning; giving in.

"But we have ridden Rose of Sharon," said Sally to Thalia as they stood at the end of the lane waiting for Mr Lorimer to pick them up and take them to the rehearsal.

"I know," said Thalia, "but we should be riding in the pageant. We should have been Nick's pages. We should. Now we'll probably never see him again."

Nick had been discussing his arrangements with Mr Frazer and Lady Muriel. He was driving down to the Borders to jump Gemini, one of his other horses, in a show, leaving Rosie at Mr Frazer's. Driving back up very early the next day for the pageant, probably arriving about seven and after the pageant taking Rosie straight back home.

So Sally could see that Thalia was probably right. They wouldn't really see Nick or Rosie again. Only a glimpse of them at the pageant. Next time would be on TV.

"We should be riding in it," nagged Thalia, refusing to be comforted. "Should! Should! Should!"

The Lorimers' car drove up. It was over-loaded already with costumes, picnic, all the Lorimers, except the Beardies, and Thalia's Narg.

"There's no room for you," said Mr Lorimer who had rearranged his shifts in the library giving him the day off. "But squeeze in. If the police see us we've had it."

Mrs Lorimer had shopping to do before she went to Torbracken so Sally, Thalia, Em and Ben were dropped off at Torbracken's gates.

"I'll take my pike and my sword," said Ben. "I don't want Jamie messing about with them."

They walked slowly up the drive, not wanting to be too early. Em practising her song, Thalia telling Ben how unfair it all was and Sally imagining she was cantering along on Rose of Sharon.

There was the ring of trotting hooves coming along the road, sounding like a battalion of horse. They slowed down and turned into the drive. As they came closer Sally looked back. They were, as she had known they would be, the mounted followers from Mr Frazer's stables.

They filled the whole drive, forcing Thalia and the Lorimers into the rhododendrons. At the back of the cavalcade was Charlotte on her piebald. She was talking to an older woman on a finely bred bay.

"That's her," Charlotte said in a loud voice, pointing to Sally. "It was only a tiny toss and she would not get on again. And now she seems to think she can barge her way into the stables and be in everything. Lady Muriel sorted her out."

They rode past, leaving Sally scarlet-faced and furious.

When they reached Torbracken House the Scouts took over. Battlers, dancers, foot followers and crowd were swiftly sorted out. Sally and Thalia were sent to get their crowd costumes from a huge room in Torbracken House, where trestle tables laden with second-hand clothes mingled with suits of armour and dead animal heads hanging from the walls.

"Now dears, are you specials?" asked a plump, white haired lady in charge of one of the tables.

"We should be. . ." began Thalia.

"No," said Sally, past caring.

"Crowd, general," said the lady and burrowed into the piles of clothes, coming out with floral skirts which she girded round them and patterned sheets which she knotted round their shoulders to act as shawls.

"There," she said, setting a straw hat covered with wilting silken roses on top of

Thalia's fizzing hair. "You'll come wearing them for the pageant and hand them back before you leave."

All afternoon the sun blazed down as Thalia, Sally and some thirty others who were crowd were chivvied around the walled garden. First they were to come out of Torbracken House to be crowd watching the dancing and singing, then terrified crowd watching while the battle raged. Next sullen crowd muttering amongst themselves when the king almost knighted the wrong man and last of all cheering crowd when the true owner of Torbracken was knighted.

Three times Sally and Thalia slipped away to where they could hear the horses and battlers being drilled by Lady Muriel and the organizing man. Twice they were spotted by Daisy and the third time Lady Muriel threatened to ban them from the pageant altogether if she saw them again.

Thalia squared her shoulders and scowled up at Lady Muriel, ready to answer back. But Sally gripped her by the sleeve and pulled her away.

"If she bans us we'll not even see Nick at

the pageant," Sally said, dragging Thalia away to be crowd again.

In the evening they rode their ponies bareback along the sands, following the crimpling line of the waves.

"But it is so unfair," mourned Thalia. "It is not fair."

"I know," Sally agreed, but there did not seem to be anything they could do about it.

Chapter Eight

All night long Sally tossed and turned. In her dreams Charlotte had stolen Willow and was riding in the pageant with Nick. In her darkest nightmares Sally watched Nick galloping Rosie round and round, leaping clean over Torbracken House with Lady Muriel following him mounted on a black horse and cackling with evil laughter.

It was half past three when Sally woke properly. She sat straight up in bed, for a second she could hardly think who she was and then she remembered her last dream. It had been about the crystal unicorn.

Sally leapt out of bed, ran across to where her riding jacket was hanging behind the door and searched through the pockets till she found the unicorn. She could not understand how she had forgotten about it again. Sitting on the window seat, her knees under her chin, her nightdress tucked under her toes, Sally looked quietly down at the glittering crystal unicorn; its green, scarlet eyes; its golden horn. Beyond the window grey sea stretched to grey sky. Only the unicorn in her hand glinted and shimmered.

"Unicorn, horn of light, show me the way." Sally spoke aloud, the words forming themselves, without her having to think them first.

And instantly Sally knew what she would do. She would go and wake Thalia and they would ride over to the stables to say goodbye to Rosie.

Sally scrambled into her clothes, crept downstairs, resisted the appealing eyes of the Beardies and once outside raced down to the ponies' field.

Thalia was standing at the gate.

"How did you know?" demanded Sally, staring at Thalia in utter amazement.

"I woke up suddenly and the only thing

in my head was to go and see Rosie. I was coming to wake you."

"It was the unicorn," said Sally, taking it out of her anorak pocket. "I was holding it in my hand and I just knew that I had to come and get you and ride to the stables."

Both girls stood staring down at the unicorn lying in the palm of Sally's hand until Tarquin came trotting to the gate, whinnying – breaking the spell.

"It's really very early," said Sally cautiously.

"So there will be no one to see us," said Thalia.

They rode across the sands, trotting to begin with and then at a canter that changed to a gallop as if something were forcing them on, as if they were riding on some urgent mission.

"But we're not only riding to see Rosie," Sally thought, not knowing why she was crouching tight and close over her pony's withers, urging her on.

"I think," Thalia said when the stables came into sight, "there's a back way in. If we go up onto the road someone might see us."

Remembering Betsy and her foal and the noise the ponies made when they were ridden past her, Sally agreed and followed Thalia round the fields towards the back of the stables.

There was no sound. The ponies' hooves were muffled in the sand; no gulls' cries; no traffic on the road. Far to early for anyone but themselves to be up.

"Think this is the place," said Thalia and rode Tarquin across the scrubby ground to where a hawthorn hedge grew along the bottom of one of Mr Frazer's fields. "Yes, this is it."

But Sally, riding behind Thalia, couldn't see a gate. There was a gap in the hedge blocked with crossed poles but no gate.

"I'll go first," said Thalia and instantly Sally realized that she was going to jump the poles.

"You can't!" Sally exclaimed. "You can't! It's far too high."

"Rubbish! We've jumped higher than that in the paddock. We're only jumping into the field. It's quite flat. Willow will clear it easily. Jump behind me."

"I can't," began Sally, pulling on Willow's reins, trying to hold her back. The crossed poles seemed enormous – the height of a jump at the White City.

"Oh stop," gasped Sally but Thalia and Tarquin were cantering at the poles. Sally stared, wide-eyed, in total panic, as Tarquin leaped, clearing the poles easily and landing far out into the field.

Willow's ears were sharp; her hooves trampling the ground as she danced to follow Tarquin.

"Come on!" yelled Thalia.

With a half-rear Willow bounded forward. Sally clutched at her mane, all Martine's teaching totally forgotten. Willow raced at the jump, got in too close, shot straight into the air, throwing Sally out of the saddle. When they landed Sally fell forward onto Willow's neck. For a second Sally was sure she was coming off, but somehow, digging with her elbow into Willow's shoulder, clutching desperately at her fistful of mane, she managed to struggle back into the saddle.

"What did you do that for?" demanded Thalia scornfully. "You were nearly off."

Sally was too mad with herself to answer. She knew it had all been her fault. If she had ridden Willow at the jump, letting her canter on, remembering Martine's instruction to throw your heart over the jump, Willow would have jumped every bit as well as Tarquin.

"I think that's the box Rosie is in," said Thalia as they rode along the side of a high hedge that led towards the stables and she pointed to a large loosebox standing a little way apart from the range of stabling.

Three oak trees grew at the end of the hedge, just before the gate. Thalia and Sally had almost reached the trees when they heard the sound of a heavy vehicle being driven into the stableyard. Sally looked at her watch. It was only twenty past four, too early for anyone to be up and about at the stables.

They halted their ponies and waited, hidden by the trees. To their surprise the engine didn't stop in the stableyard but came on to the space in front of Rosie's box.

Standing up in their stirrups they saw a huge horse box with a Clydesdale horse painted on its side. Jumping down from the cabin came two men. One was tall and angular with stooped shoulders, red hair and a red beard. He looked around him with a shifty expression in his bullet eyes and his long nose sniffed the air as if he was searching for something; something that he intended to find no matter what the cost.

The other man was about twenty-five, unshaved with dirty, fair hair and a blank expression. They were both dressed in shabby clothes. The older man had a dirty raincoat belted over tweed trousers and the young man was wearing an ancient tweed jacket, torn and stained, jeans and green wellingtons.

"What do they want?" Thalia mouthed.

Sally lifted eyebrows and shoulders to signal that she had no idea.

The men waited for a few minutes by the horsebox cabin, talking in low tones, then walked over to Rosie's box.

"If they go in to Rosie I'll stay here, you go and get Mr Frazer," organized Thalia in an urgent whisper.

"Do you think they're going to steal her?"

Thalia nodded violently and then to their total amazement Martine came from behind the row of looseboxes and hurried across the yard to the men. They stood for a moment talking to each other then Martine went into the loosebox and the two men let down the ramp of the horsebox.

"Go and get Mr Frazer," mouthed Thalia.

"Can't. Not when it's Martine, too."

In minutes Martine had led Rosie out of her box and loaded her into the horse box. The ramp soared skywards, shutting her in. The two men and Martine climbed into the cabin and the box was driven out of the yard.

"Where are they taking her?" demanded Sally. "Nick's coming for her here on the morning of the pageant. Why have they taken her away?"

"They've stolen her," stated Thalia.

"Not Martine!"

"You saw her. She's in on it too. A show jumper like Rosie would be worth thousands of pounds.

"But Martine wouldn't do a thing like that."

"We've seen her. Come on, we've got to follow them. Find out where they're taking her."

"We'll never catch up with them."

"It's Mr Stamford's horsebox. He uses Clydesdales on his farm. Bet they're taking her there. Come on, it's not too far from here."

Thalia jumped off Tarquin, opened the field gate and in no time they were cantering along the grass verge of the road to Stamford's farm.

"This way," called Thalia and they turned down a track that led along the edge of a field of crops, looped round a hill of rough grazing and in front of them was a low-lying farmhouse cushioned in sycamore trees. They skirted round the hill until they could see the back of the farm and there in the yard was the horsebox. There was no sign of any humans as they rode down closer to the farm.

"If anyone comes out they're bound to see us," said Sally. Her imagination was filled with visions of the red bearded man and the fair headed man pouncing on them, dragging them off their ponies and leaving them bound and gagged while they took Rosie away, never to be seen again.

They rode downhill towards the farm and

had just reached the shelter of a high stone wall when they heard voices. Jumping down from their ponies they each found a spy hole between the stones.

"He'll never find her there," said the red bearded man.

"Never," laughed Martine.

"That'll teach him," agreed the younger man.

Through her crack Sally was just able to see Martine closing the top door of a loose box on Rosie and turning to walk away with the two men, back to the farm.

"They have stolen her," whispered Thalia. "Bet they don't leave her here for long. She'll be on a plane tonight. Probably take her to America or sell her to some Arab sheik."

"But not Martine," Sally protested.

"Come on, let's go in and speak to Rosie," said Thalia, ignoring Sally. "We've got to let her know we're here."

They knotted their reins over their ponies' necks and left them by the side of the wall. Then they climbed over a gate, made a frantic dash across the yard, opened the box door just wide enough to let themselves in and quickly shut it again once they were inside. Tight with nerves they waited to see if anyone had seen them, but there was no sound of footsteps or voices.

Rosie pricked her ears, lowered her great white head and blew over their hair.

"It's all right," said Sally, stretching up to clap Rosie's neck. "Nick will be back tomorrow. We'll tell him where you are."

"Don't be so soft," hissed Thalia. "We can't leave her here! They'll be back for her. Think of Shergar. They horseknapped him and no one ever saw him again."

"We could tell my dad."

"And he'd tell the police and then what would happen to Martine?"

Dust motes danced in a beam of light from a window high in the roof; the good smells of hay and horse filled the air. Rose of Sharon loomed above them, huge and white in the gloom.

"We've got to do something," said Thalia desperately. "And we've got to do it now."

"Take her to Kestrels," said Sally, for it was the only way: the only way they could be sure of keeping Rosie safe for Nick.

Chapter Nine

"At last!" exclaimed Thalia. It seemed to have taken them ages to put on Rosie's tack and every second they had been sure that someone would come in and find them.

"Kestrels, here we come."

For a second they hesitated.

"Say they catch us," Sally thought. "What if someone sees us before we get home? What would Dad say? Would the police think we'd stolen her? Say she gets away and causes an accident or injures herself?"

But Thalia had already taken the reins over Rosie's head and was opening the box door.

"Shut it behind us," Thalia said as Rosie burst out of the box into the yard.

She stood staring about her, a massive mountain of horse. Her crested neck and bulked shoulders were high above Thalia's head as she led her across the yard, through the gate and into the field.

When Rosie saw Tarquin and Willow she whinnied with a sound of thunder and the two ponies came trotting towards her, Tarquin giving sharp, pig-squeals of delight as Rosie, dragging Thalia behind her, stormed to meet him.

"Catch him," yelled Thalia. "Get them away from Rosie. I can't hold her!"

Sally grabbed the reins of both ponies.

"Get on," she urged, running ahead and trying to drag the ponies with her. "Leave Rosie alone. Get on with you."

Willow trotted obediently forward but Tarquin, half-rearing, fought to get to Rosie. Grasping both reins, Sally was stretched out between the two ponies while Thalia hung on to Rosie's reins with both hands.

"I can't hold her!" Thalia screamed desperately.

Sally swung Willow round and yelling and hauling at Tarquin managed to drag them both off the track and into the field.

"It's no good," shouted Thalia who was still anchoring Rosie by hanging onto her bit ring, "You'll need to ride them."

But when Sally rode Willow and led Tarquin it wasn't any better. Twice Tarquin dragged his reins out of Sally's grasp and trotted back to Rosie, trapping Thalia in a fury of stamping hooves and reaching teeth.

The second time Thalia managed to drag Tarquin away from Rosie and give his reins back to Sally she was close to tears.

"We can't go on like this," she said. "Someone's going to get hurt. I don't want Tarquin kicked and lamed, even if it is by a world famous showjumper," and she glared at Rosie, almost hating her.

"Could I take Rosie?" Sally suggested.

"Might as well try. We must get back to Kestrels before there are any cars on the road or someone is bound to see us."

In a muddle of reins they changed over. In minutes Thalia had mounted Tarquin and, heels sharp against his sides, hands hard on his reins, had him paying attention to her while Willow walked mildly at his side.

Grasping Rosie's reins Sally followed behind, Rosie high-stepping at her side. Her neck was arched and she clinked her bit impatiently, shaking her head against Sally's feeble hold.

They were almost round the hill when a hare leapt up at Rosie's feet. She sprang to the side, rearing, dragging Sally off her feet; then she leapt forward blundering into Tarquin and Willow. Tarquin bucked furiously, dumping Thalia onto the ground.

Sally felt Rosie's reins scorching through her hands and she and the two ponies were free.

In seconds the ponies and Rosie were high-tailing it over the hill while Sally stood blowing on her hand and Thalia struggled to her feet.

"Come on," screamed Thalia. "We've got to catch them before Rosie breaks a leg."

Running full out they raced over the hillside to where Rosie and the ponies were standing watching them. They had almost reached them when Tarquin flung up his heels and with the other two following, galloped back towards the farm. Sally and Thalia raced after them. Again they stormed off over the hillside just as the girls got close.

"It's no use," cried Thalia. "We'll never catch them this way. Never!"

"Someone's bound to come out and see us," said Sally. "We've got to catch them."

"We'll walk backwards," said Thalia. "Then they'll think we're going away from them."

Stumbling over the rough ground they approached backwards. Rosie and the two ponies stood with their heads low, ears pricked, staring suspiciously at this strange behaviour.

"When I say now, we dash and grab," mouthed Thalia.

They walked backwards until Sally was certain they were going to bump into the ponies.

"Are you ready?" demanded Thalia.

Sally gulped and nodded.

"Now," breathed Thalia.

They sprang round and flung themselves at the horses but they were far too slow. With Rosie leading they plunged away.

"We'll never. . ." began Sally.

"We've got them," screamed Thalia and raced towards the ponies.

As they had galloped off Tarquin's stirrup had become entangled with Willow's stirrup leather. Both ponies were standing stock still, neither able to understand what was holding them back. Even when Sally grasped Willow's reins and Thalia closed her hand on Tarquin's bridle, they did not move.

Quickly Thalia untwisted the stirrups.

"You are the most foul, horrendous horror," she told Tarquin in tones of loving kindness.

"But Rosie?" asked Sally anxiously.

"Perhaps she'll follow them," suggested Thalia.

They turned and led their ponies away and Rosie, with a trumpeting whinny, came stamping after them. Her front feet thundering the ground as she reared beside them. Sally felt Rosie's reins swing against her arm and grabbed. For a second the white mare plunged backwards almost pulling Sally off her feet. Then she stood still, blowing through wide nostrils.

"Cor," said Thalia. "Thought you'd had it."

They stood staring at each other, knowing that anything could have happened to the horses in their mad galloping.

"What are we going to do now?" asked Thalia desperately. "How are we ever going to get back to Kestrels? They can't carry on like this on the road."

"You could ride Rosie," said a voice in Sally's head and at once she knew why Rosie had seemed so familiar. One of the dream horses Sally had ridden before she found Willow had been Lucia – a white mare as proud and as powerful as Rose of Sharon. That was why she had wanted to canter Rosie; that was why she had not been afraid.

"I'll ride Rosie," said Sally. "You'll need to give me a leg-up."

"You can't! Not on the road! She might run off with you. Rear or shy or anything."

"She won't," said Sally. "She knows me. Honestly we'll be okay."

Because she couldn't think of anything else to do Thalia agreed and gave Sally a leg-up; pulling at the saddle Sally scrambled astride the white mare.

"We'll go first," Sally said when she had sorted out her stirrups.

And hardly giving Thalia time to get on Tarquin, Rosie broke into a drumming trot.

Sally made no attempt to hold her back. She had never checked Lucia and now she let Rosie have her head. They cantered up the track by the cornfield and when they reached the road Rosie turned willingly in the direction of Kestrels and cantered along the verge.

There was nothing in Sally's world but the power of her dream horse, now real in the form of Rose of Sharon.

As they approached Kestrels Sally tightened her reins and Rosie bumped into a trot and then a walk. Sally rode her through Kestrels' gateway and waited in the drive for Thalia to catch up.

"You went like the hammers," cried Thalia. "If Nick could have seen you! These two are knackered."

Seeing Willow blowing and sweating made Sally suddenly conscious of the real world again.

"Better get Rosie into a box," said Thalia,

and Sally walked her down the drive towards the black tower of Kestrels. Now it was Rose of Sharon she was riding; Lucia had vanished.

There was still no sign of life in Kestrels, even Misty did not bark when they passed the house on their way to the stables.

When they had settled Rosie, giving her water and hay, they shut the top half of the loose box door on her. They rubbed down their own ponies and left them in their boxes, afraid to turn them out in case Rosie made a fuss about being left alone.

"Now what?" demanded Thalia.

"Food," said Sally. "We'll have a picnic out here to avoid questions."

There was no one in the kitchen so Sally searched through the cupboards and returned to Thalia with bread, butter, cold cheese and potato pie, half a bowl of jelly and lemonade.

But even when they'd eaten things weren't any better.

"One thing is certain," said Thalia. "We've got to keep her here until Nick comes back tomorrow."

"Say they come looking for her? Martine and those two men?"

"They would never think of coming here," stated Thalia with total optimism.

"But say the police come?"

"Bet you they won't have gone to the police. That's the last place they would go. It's your parents who mustn't see her."

"Usually they only come down in the evening to check that everything is all right. Perhaps they won't notice. They're pretty blind."

Later, when Sally and Thalia went into Kestrels, Sally asked her mother if Thalia could stay the night.

"Of course, if it's okay with Narg," said Mrs Lorimer, her head full of plans for the pageant – costumes, food, Jamie (who was not being allowed to be a Battler and had to be amused) Beardies, Mr Lorimer's sword which still had to be made and Em's special costume because she was singing.

"We thought we would keep the ponies in, so they'll be clean for tomorrow. I know we can't ride them in the pageant but we might just ride them *to* the pageant and we'd want them to look smart."

"As long as you don't cause any more trouble with the old lady," said Mrs Lorimer.

"We won't," said Sally vaguely.

Thalia went to ask her Narg if it would be all right if she stayed with Sally. Em and Sally washed up and tidied their rooms. Quickly Sally twitched her things away into drawers and wardrobe. Settled her duvet onto her bed. Threw herself down on top of it and thought, "We have Rose of Sharon in our stable. I rode her here," and shivered with delight. But there wasn't time to lie and daydream about it. Sally jumped back up and raced down to the stables to listen outside Rosie's door to make sure she was still there.

When Thalia came back, they groomed their ponies, although their plans of riding to the pageant in the hope of joining in were forgotten. Nothing mattered now except to let Nick know that they had his showjumper.

"Tell me again," said Thalia when they were both sitting in the yard cleaning their tack, "the exact words you heard Nick saying to Mr Frazer."

"I've told you about ten times already and

you must have heard him yourself," Sally said, but it did not stop her going over it again. It seemed the only thing worth doing to fill in the minutes that lumbered past like hours. "Nick said he would be driving up first thing tomorrow morning. He would go straight to Mr Frazer's and that he expected to be there about seven."

"We've got to stop him getting there," said Thalia. We've got to catch him and tell him that Rosie is safe."

Morning crept into afternoon.

"Whatever happens we must catch him before he reaches the stables. If he finds Rosie isn't there, Nick will go straight to the police. Then what would happen to Martine?" Sally repeated for the umpteenth time.

Every hour on the hour they went in to see Rosie, to fill up her water bucket and give her more hay.

"Hope this is right," said Sally as she filled the hay net yet again.

"Won't matter for one day. Not as if it's oats. Nick can sort it out tomorrow."

"If we catch him," said Sally as they left Rosie alone again to stand placidly dozing, paying no attention to Tarquin roistering around in the next-door box.

In the evening only Ben came to tell them it was time to go in and to ask if the ponies were all right. He was far too excited at the thought of being a battler to notice the closed box door or hear the sound of heavy, most-definitely-not-pony-hooves on the stone floor.

When they went up to bed Thalia said it would be best if they sat up and kept their clothes on for the morning, so that whenever the alarm went off they would be ready. Sally agreed and set the alarm for five o'clock so they would be certain to be at the crossroads for six.

After an hour of sitting up it seemed more sensible to lie down under the duvet. In a few moments they were both asleep.

The alarm rang at five, making Sally turn over and Thalia hide her face in the pillow, but neither of them woke up.

Chapter Ten

It was Misty who woke them, scratching at the door to get in.

"Half-past six," screamed Thalia, grabbing Sally and shaking her awake. "We'll be too late for Nick."

Still drugged with sleep they staggered into the bathroom, then pulled on jodh. boots, grabbed up hard hats and hurtled downstairs, banging the back door in Misty's face.

They had hardly arrived at the crossroads when Nick's brilliant yellow car scorched towards them.

"Nick STOP! Nick Ross STOP! STOP! STOP!" they screamed, standing up in their stirrups, waving wildly, ready to gallop after Nick if he didn't stop.

The car roared past them, then with a screech of brakes it skidded to a halt.

"What the dickens are you two at now?" demanded Nick, sticking his head out of the car window and looking in blank amazement as Sally and Thalia rode down upon him, both shouting at once.

"They tried to steal her," garbled Thalia. "But we stopped them. We saved her."

"She's at Kestrels. She's quite safe. We rescued her for you."

When Nick had calmed them down and managed to make out that Rosie was at Sally's house he said he would drive on and meet them there. Then they could explain exactly what had happened.

When Sally and Thalia reached Kestrels, Nick had parked half-way down the drive.

"Follow us," said Sally. "And could you be as quiet as possible because my family don't know about Rosie."

"I hope you kids have got a good explanation for all this."

"They were stealing her," said Thalia. "And *we* saved her for you."

Nick started to ask another question but changed his mind. "Right. On you go," he said impatiently.

Sally and Thalia led the way past Kestrels and round to the stables. They jumped off their ponies and rushed them into their boxes but by the time they had shut them in Nick was in with Rosie – clapping her, talking to her and checking her over in case anything had happened to her.

"Now," he said, looking up sharply. "Let's have it."

"They were stealing her," began Thalia.

"Who?" interrupted Nick.

"Two men," said Sally and sent a dagger look at Thalia warning her not to mention Martine. "They took her to Stamford's farm. We followed them and brought Rosie here."

"If it hadn't been for us she might have been in America by now," said Thalia, who thought Nick was not being as grateful as he should have been.

"Stamford's farm?" asked Nick. "And what were the two men like?"

"One had red hair and a red beard and was tall and round-shouldered. The other had fairish hair and was young," said Thalia.

"I thought as much," said Nick and suddenly he was roaring with laughter. "The bad old rascal. And I'll bet you Martine had a hand in it too!"

"What's so funny?" demanded Thalia.

"Because. . ." began Nick but couldn't speak for laughing. "Because. . ."

"I don't think it's funny," said Sally. "You might never have seen Rosie again."

"Sorry," gasped Nick. "I might have known they'd be up to something. Listen, your thieves were Lady Muriel's son and grandson."

"They couldn't have been!" exclaimed Thalia. "They were real villains and filthy dirty. You should have seen them".

"But that's who they were. Their idea of a joke. Scrobble Rosie. Wait for me to arrive back. No Rosie. Thomas, that's the grandson, would have taken my place in the pageant which was what he wanted to do. When I was over at Torbracken he was moaning on about being the rightful heir and how he should be in the pageant not me."

"You mean it was all a joke? Rosie was safe all the time?" demanded Thalia, hardly able to believe what Nick was saying.

"It wasn't easy rescuing her," said Sally. "And all the time she didn't need rescuing."

"Oh but she did!" exclaimed Nick. "Now we've got her here we can show them what's what. They will have been going crazy trying to phone me to tell me that Rosie had vanished but they wouldn't be able to get me because I changed my plans, stayed at a different place."

"Are you going to tell them you've found her now?" asked Thalia.

"Not likely. I am going to phone Auntie Mu. No one will be up, so I'll leave a message on her answer phone telling her that I've been delayed and would they bring Rosie to the pageant. Of course they won't be able to because she's here, so – panic, panic, panic. But the pageant will go on. I'm certain Thomas will be geared up to take my part, so we are going to ride over, wait hidden in the pine trees until we get a signal that the battle is over and the evil steward has been sorted out. Then as the king is about to knight the real owner – played by Thomas – we will gallop into the walled garden, expose Thomas for the twister he is and claim Torbracken as ours!"

"We?" demanded Thalia. "You and Rosie?"

"Thought you were both mad keen to ride in the pageant? Or have you changed your minds?"

"Of course we want to ride in it!" exclaimed Thalia.

"You mean we can ride with you?" cried Sally.

"Must have pages. Can't be a rightful owner without two pages," and Nick went out to his car to phone Lady Muriel.

"All fixed," he said, coming back to them. "Message left on the answer phone. Total confusion will follow," and Nick clapped Rosie, pulling her long ears through his hands, chuckling in delight.

"Wait till Charlotte sees us," said Thalia, gloating at the thought.

"Now, might your parents oblige with some coffee? Then I'll exercise Rosie and then we'll make our plans."

When Nick had been introduced to the Lorimers, finished his coffee and toast and gone out to Rosie, Mr Lorimer gave Sally and Thalia a hard look.

"Perhaps," he said, "there is a little explaining to be done about your part in all this. Why didn't you tell us about it?"

"We couldn't," said Sally. "In case you told the police and they accused Martine."

"We were sure they'd all stolen Rosie. It was not funny then," declared Thalia.

"You *should* have told us," said Mrs Lorimer. "We'll discuss it later. Did Nick say you'd need costumes?"

"Sort of tabards to wear on top of our shirts, and cloaks?"

Mrs Lorimer said she had not a second to spare, that they all had to be at Torbracken for one o'clock but she would see what she could do.

While Nick was exercising Rosie, Sally and Thalia groomed their ponies and gave their tack a quick rub over.

When Nick came back they all sat down round the kitchen table.

"Listen carefully," said Nick, grinning round at everyone. "This is it:

"Sally and Thalia and I will ride along

116

the back lanes to Torbracken. We'll go in through the farm and wait at the edge of the pine trees. The pageant starts at three, doesn't it?"

"Yes," said Em. "That's when I'm on. There are peasants and servants from the house watching the dancing, and I sing and then it's the battle."

"Could you slip away whenever the battle starts and come and let us know as fast as possible?"

"Easy," said the newest member of the Nick Ross fan club.

"Well done," said Nick. "So there's the battle, then the king and his mounted followers return to knight the owner of Torbracken House. He nearly knights the evil steward but just in time Thomas will ride in as the real owner of Torbracken. That's when we must gallop in through the formal gardens, just before he is knighted and I shall give that Thomas what for! I'll teach him to lay a finger on my Rosie."

"You'll need to get your timing spot on," said Mr Lorimer. "No use if Thomas is knighted before you arrive."

"Don't worry, we'll be there," laughed Nick and he sprang to his feet, waving an imaginary sword round his head and calling down curses on the name of Thomas.

It wasn't until Sally was tying her red velvet, curtain-cloak round her shoulders, that she felt her stomach tighten with nerves. It had all been so sudden, changing from riding Willow to the pageant knowing that they were bound to be turned away, into riding there with Nick and Rosie to show them that Nick was better than them all, that no-one could trick him and get away with it.

Running across to the stables with Thalia, Sally stopped dead, whirled round and raced back to her room. She snatched up the crystal unicorn and buried it deep in the pocket of her jeans.

When she reached the stables Nick was mounting Rosie. He was wearing long, soft-leather thigh boots, purple hose, a gold and scarlet waistcoat over a white shirt and a black cloak.

"The game's afoot," he cried, rousing them on. "We'll show them!"

When they reached Torbracken they waited, holding their horses in the shelter of the pine trees.

"That's twenty-past three," said Nick, looking at his watch uneasily. "Thought your sister would have been here by now. Better get up."

They mounted and rode to the edge of the pines. From Willow's back Sally could see Torbracken grounds, teas being served in the courtyard, six sheep in a pen, a group of archers carrying their targets, and further away the crumbled down walls of the walled garden. But there was no sign of Em.

"Nearly half-past," said Nick. "Even Auntie Mu's timing couldn't be as bad as this."

Suddenly Sally saw Em. She was holding her long skirt up round her knees and running full pelt towards the pine trees.

"Here she is," yelled Thalia, pulling up her girths while Sally eased her hard hat which was suddenly too tight and felt her stirrups hopelessly uneven.

"Couldn't get away," Em gasped. "You'll need to go *now*. Quick. At once. Or you'll be too late."

Not waiting for Em to finish Nick was cantering Rosie out onto the lawns. He rode her as if she had been a snow plough, sweeping people away before him. Sally and Thalia rode in his wake.

"Got to get there in time," Thalia muttered, sending Tarquin flying after Rosie. "Got to show them that Nick is best."

They came to a rise in the land and could just see down into the walled garden. Thomas was dismounting from a bay horse. Charlotte, holding her own piebald's reins in one hand was ready to take Thomas's reins in the other. The evil steward lay on the ground apparently dead. The king held his unsheathed sword in his hand.

They were too late. There was absolutely no way they could ride round through the formal gardens before Thomas was knighted.

"Need to jump," cried Nick "Are you fit?"

"Course," yelled Thalia, tightening her reins, making Tarquin dance, spring-heeled, ready to jump the moon.

Sally gazed terror-stricken at the wall. Fallen stones lay in mossy heaps on the side facing them and she knew that on the other side were more cascades of stone and the breadth of the flower border. She remembered how she had nearly fallen off when she had jumped into Mr Frazer's field.

Never could she jump it. Never. Never. She longed to shout, "No! No! It's too high, too broad. I'm not jumping it." But her mouth was frozen. The words weren't there.

"Keep behind me and jump where I jump," Nick shouted, standing up in his stirrups. For a moment he looked back over his shoulder, bright and fearless, tossing down his challenge to Thalia and Sally, daring them to follow where he led.

And as if there was some sort of electricity about Nick, a force that energized her whole being, Sally stopped being afraid. She remembered the unicorn in her pocket.

Sally saw Nick gather Rosie together; was aware of astonished faces staring up at them; saw Rosie pound her hooves into the earth and rise like a snow storm, soaring over the fallen stones, rising over the wall.

"Right," breathed Thalia. "Keep together."

And there was no thought in Sally's head except to follow Nick. Martine's voice clear in her head, she paced Willow towards the wall; felt without hesitation the exact moment when Willow took off and, almost without knowing it, she bent her waist, going with her pony. She felt Willow rise, soar and stretch out; saw Thalia land at her side and Nick already galloping across the walled garden.

It was like the moment when you knew you could swim or ride a bike. Sally knew she could jump.

Nick pulled Rose of Sharon to a rearing halt. The king's uplifted sword fell to the ground.

"Nick!" gasped Thomas from where he knelt in front of the king. "How did you get here? Where did you find Rosie?"

"Avaunt you scullion," roared Nick, making Rosie rear again. "Foul varlet! Squalid thief! I have you now," and leaping down from Rosie, Nick drew his sword and raged at Thomas.

Thomas lifted his arms to protect his face, shouting at Nick to stop it, that it had all been a joke.

"Joke? I'll give you joke," and Nick thwacked Thomas with the flat of his sword until he struggled to his feet and ran up the middle of the walled garden, caught his foot on a hoofprint and measured his length on the grass.

Nick grabbed him up, threw him over Rosie's withers, then jumping onto Rosie, galloped round the garden waving his sword above his head.

The people watching cheered and clapped, demanding a second lap of honour and Nick rode round triumphantly for a second time.

"You're next," Thalia threatened Charlotte. "Apologize to Sally. Promise you'll stop that stupid giggling."

Charlotte hesitated, saying nothing.

"Go on," said Thalia. "Apologize now or else. . ."

As Nick came galloping back, still holding Thomas securely across his saddle, Charlotte garbled out an apology.

"I'm sorry. I didn't mean to say anything. I'll not giggle again. I won't laugh or anything like that."

"See and remember then. Because Nick will be coming back and he'll deal with you."

When everything was over, Sally and Thalia, because they were with Nick, found themselves in the courtyard in front of Torbracken House. Battlers, followers, archers, sheep and sheepdogs and crowd of all kinds were making their way home, and Lady Muriel was serving champagne to family and friends.

"Lemonade for the kids," requested Nick, ignoring Thalia's suggestion that they would not object to champagne.

"Well done everybody. Jolly well done, I say. This day has brought destruction to all woodworm. Thanks to you all," said Lady Muriel.

Nick, Thomas, his red-bearded father, the organizing man, Martine and several other helpers raised their glasses.

"And to Nick," squeaked Sally, completely carried away by the occasion.

"Have you forgiven us?" Martine asked Nick. "Thomas was desperate to have your part. He wanted to be knighted and to be the real owner; which after all he will be some day. I could see it was a bit unfair. Just because you're famous and brilliant and were bound to draw the crowds."

"Too much," said Nick.

"It was meant to be a joke. We wanted you to arrive. No Rosie. Thomas would need to take your part."

"And say I'd gone to the police? Which I would have done immediately."

"We were going to say that we'd already told the police and that there was an officer coming to see you at the pageant. Of course there wouldn't have been but after Thomas had been knighted we were going to bring Rosie on as lost property and make you pay a fine to get her back."

"I am not amused. Under my smiling face I am furious about the whole thing. Bet you were all going crazy when you found she'd vanished."

"You could say that, but that would be putting it mildly. We couldn't reach you on the phone. We didn't want to involve the police in case the newspapers got hold of the story. Lady Muriel calmed us down. Said she was sure you were at the bottom of it and the best thing we could do was wait until you arrived."

"All Auntie Mu would be thinking about would be her bloomin' pageant," said Nick.

"Could be," agreed Martine. "But you'll never know how relieved I was to see you jumping over that wall on Rosie."

"I can imagine," said Nick grinning.

Thomas's father came up and began to apologise to Nick, and Mrs Lorimer came searching for Sally and Thalia. Meg and Misty bounded at the end of their leads. Someone, probably Em, had brushed out their coats until they looked like Cruft's show dogs – pure white ruffs, paddy paws, black and grey coats, shining cascades of silken hair.

"Like your dogs," said Lady Muriel. "What breed?"

"It's Misty," said Sally in delight. "And Meg. I've told you before they are pure-bred, pedigreed, Bearded Collies!"

Lady Muriel honked in disbelief.

"Time you were getting home," Mrs Lorimer said. "We're going so don't be long."

And suddenly Sally realized that it really was all over. They had ridden in the pageant with

Nick Ross, the world famous showjumper and Rose of Sharon his snow-white mare. And she knew how to jump. Knew what they meant when they told her to bend her waist. But it was over.

Nick said he had to be off smartish. He made arrangements to leave Rosie at Torbracken while he went with Thomas's father to collect his own car from Kestrels and his trailer from Mr Frazer's stables; and, promising Sally and Thalia tickets for the Horse of the Year show, he had gone.

Sally and Thalia said thank you and goodbye to anyone who was listening, mounted their ponies and walked back along the road until they came to a track that led down to the shore. Without a word they turned and rode down over the dunes towards the sea.

"Been smashing," said Thalia. "That was some jump."

"It was," agreed Sally in total satisfaction.

"D'you think he will send us tickets?"

"Might. He said he would."

But it didn't really matter, Sally thought. It had been good riding Rosie but only as a special thing. It was Willow that really mattered. Her own pony. Her pony to jump.

"Course I'd far rather have Tarquin," said Thalia, reading Sally's thoughts. "Pairs jumping at the Tarent Show cross-country? Narg's got the entry forms."

"Okay," said Sally, grinning.

"We'll probably win," laughed Thalia as they let their ponies canter on towards the high tower of Kestrels, their heads filled with thoughts of cross-country obstacles as high as the fallen wall with its spread of scattered stones.

"Red rosettes and a cup," romanced Thalia.

"Red rosettes and a cup," echoed Sally as she put her hand in her pocket and felt the crystal unicorn lying there safe and magic. "Should not be in the least surprised."